Other Books by Mitsumasa Anno
published by Philomel Books

Anno's Animals

Anno's Britain

Anno's Counting House

Anno's Flea Market

Anno's Hat Tricks

Anno's Italy

Anno's Journey

Anno's Magical ABC:
An Anamorphic Alphabet

Anno's Mysterious Multiplying Jar

Anno's U.S.A.

The King's Flower

The Unique World of Mitsumasa Anno:
Selected Works (1969–1977)

First USA edition 1986. Published by Philomel Books, a member of The Putnam Publishing Group, 51 Madison Avenue, New York, NY 10010. Text translation copyright © 1986 by Philomel Books. Original Japanese edition published by Dowaya, Tokyo, copyright © 1985 by Kuso-Kobo and Tuyosi Mori. All rights reserved. Translation rights arranged with Dowaya through the Japan Foreign-Rights Centre (JFC). Printed in Japan.

Library of Congress Cataloging-in-Publication Data. Mori, Tuyosi, 1928- . Socrates and the three little pigs. Summary: A wolf's attempt to figure out in which of five houses he is most likely to find one of the three little pigs introduces such mathematical concepts as combinatorial analysis, permutations, and probabilities. 1. Combinations—Juvenile literature. 2. Combinatorial analysis—Juvenile literature. 3. Permutations—Juvenile literature. 4. Probabilities—Juvenile literature. [1. Combinations. 2. Combinatorial analysis. 3. Permutations. 4. Probabilities] I. Anno, Mitsumasa, 1926- . II. Title. QA165.M595 1986 511'.6 85-21564 ISBN 0-399-21310-4 First impression.

SOCRATES
AND THE
THREE LITTLE PIGS

Pictures by Mitsumasa Anno · Text by Tuyosi Mori

Philomel Books
New York

Once upon a time there were 3 little pigs. Socrates the wolf often saw them playing in the field near his den. How happy they look! he thought. Socrates was a philosopher and spent a lot of time thinking and talking about things like happiness with his friend Pythagoras the frog. So much thinking and talking had made Socrates quite thin.

But Xanthippe, his wife, was rather chubby. She had no patience with thinking. She was hungry, and that made her cross. Now she pulled on the rope that was tied to Socrates' tail and asked him, "When are we going to eat?"

Socrates was still thinking about the happy little pigs.

But he knew he should be thinking about Xanthippe's dinner.

Suddenly he had an idea. Perhaps he could catch one of
the 3 little pigs for her dinner!

There were 5 houses in the meadow where the 3 pigs lived.

Now it was nighttime. The 3 little pigs would be in bed.

"It would be best to catch 1 little piggie alone," advised Pythagoras.

But which house should Socrates look in? "3 piggies, 5 houses," said Socrates. "I'll have to think about this problem in an orderly way. Let's think about the first little pig.

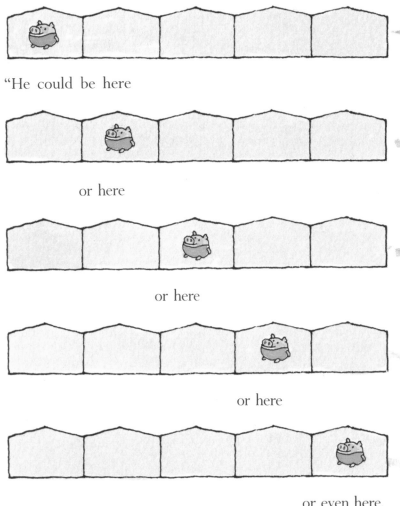

"He could be here

or here

or here

or here

or even here.

"There are 5 possible places for him to stay.

"Next let's think about the second little pig.

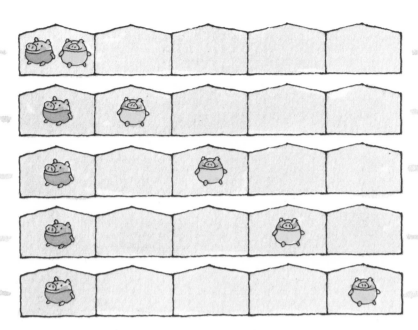

"There are also 5 possible places for him to stay.

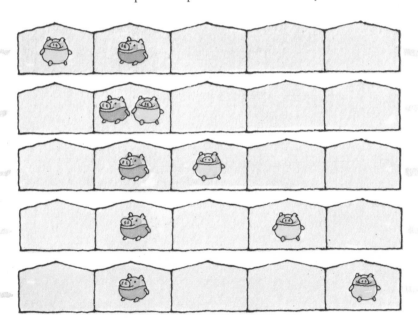

"But there seem to be some other arrangements here too.

"And then there is the third little pig. He has 5 possibilities, too. But it is getting very confusing . . ."

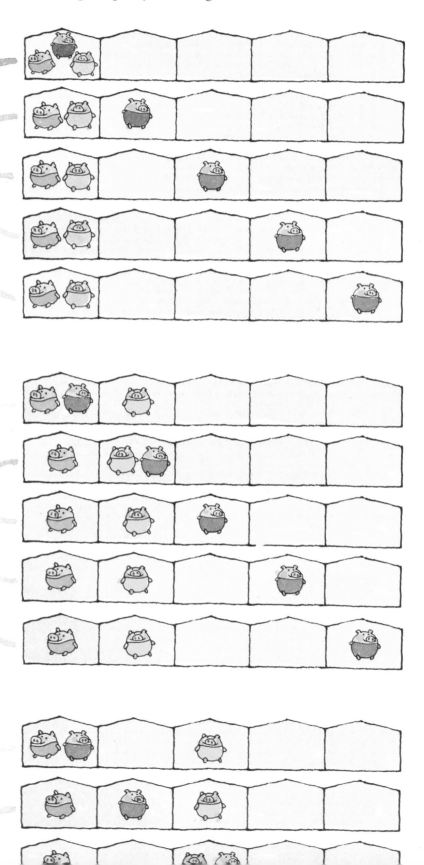

Luckily, Pythagoras the frog was a mathematician. He was very good with numbers. "Look at it this way," he told Socrates. "Here is a tree with 5 thick limbs. These are like the 5 possible houses for the first pig. At the end of each big limb there are 5 branches. These are like the possible houses for the second pig. The 5 twigs at the ends are like the 5 possible choices for the third pig. There are 5 times 5 times 5 choices, don't you see?"

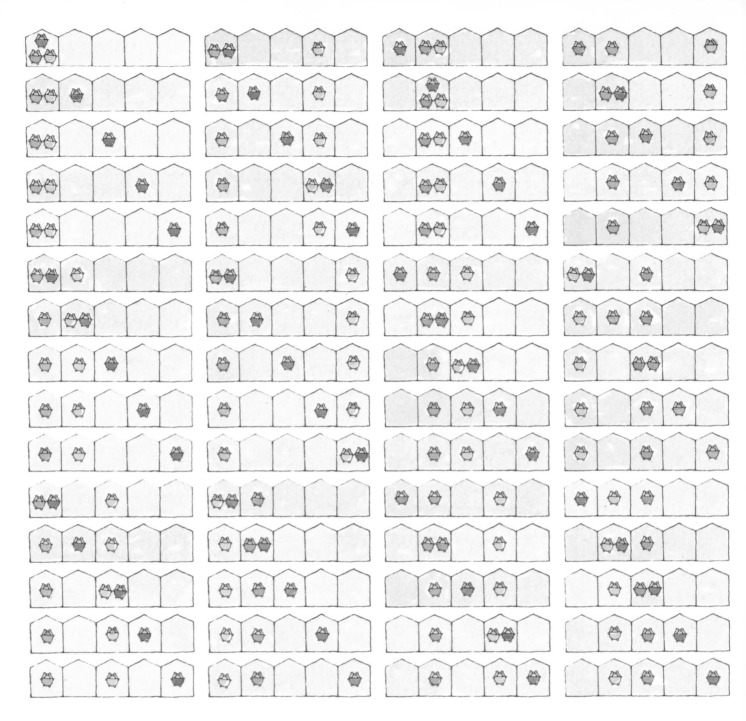

That meant 125 choices! Socrates was startled. He hadn't realized there would be so many. Where should he begin? "I think I'll draw all the different possibilities and see how it all looks. Of course, it would be simpler if we didn't care *which* pig was *where*."

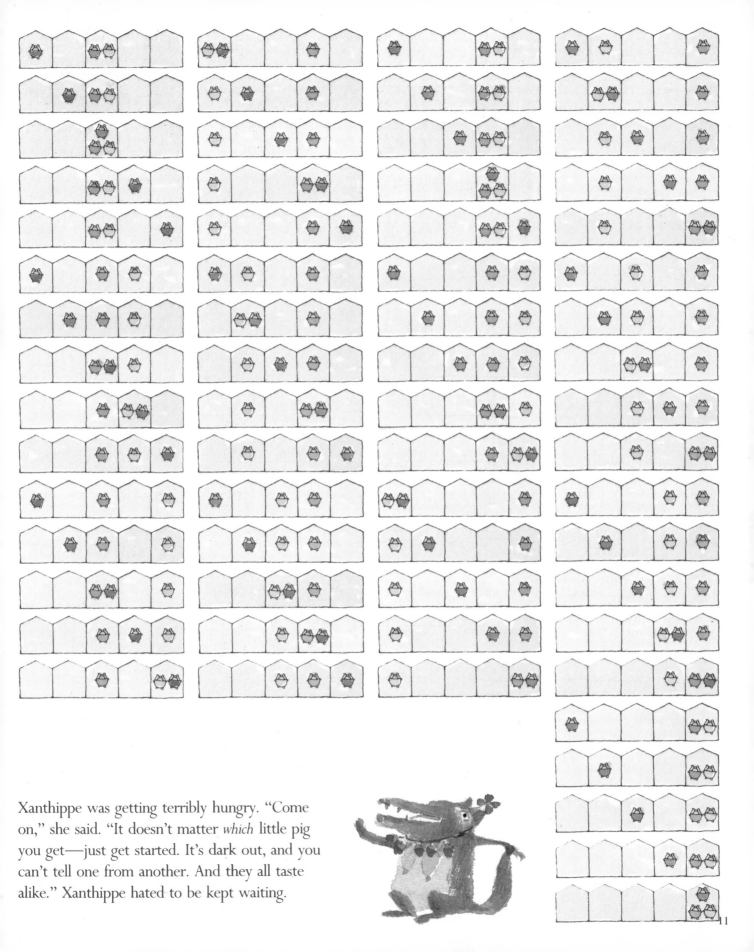

Xanthippe was getting terribly hungry. "Come on," she said. "It doesn't matter *which* little pig you get—just get started. It's dark out, and you can't tell one from another. And they all taste alike." Xanthippe hated to be kept waiting.

11

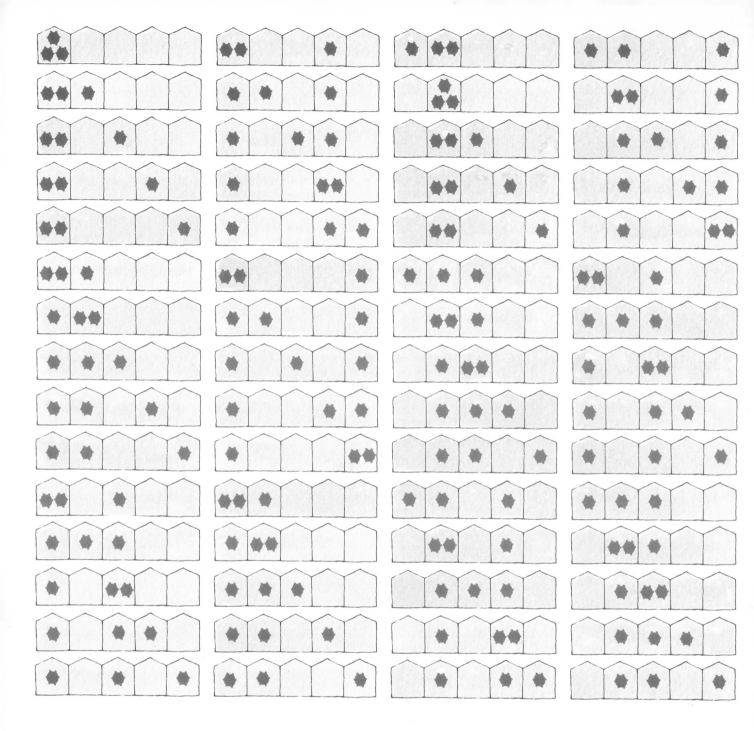

"A good point, my dear Xanthippe! We'll color them all gray," said Socrates. "But now look—there is only 1 pattern that looks like this ⬠⬠⬠⬠⬠ , but there are many that look like this ⬠⬠⬠⬠⬠ or this ⬠⬠⬠⬠⬠ . How can we figure this out, Pythagoras? Where would we be most likely to find a pig?"

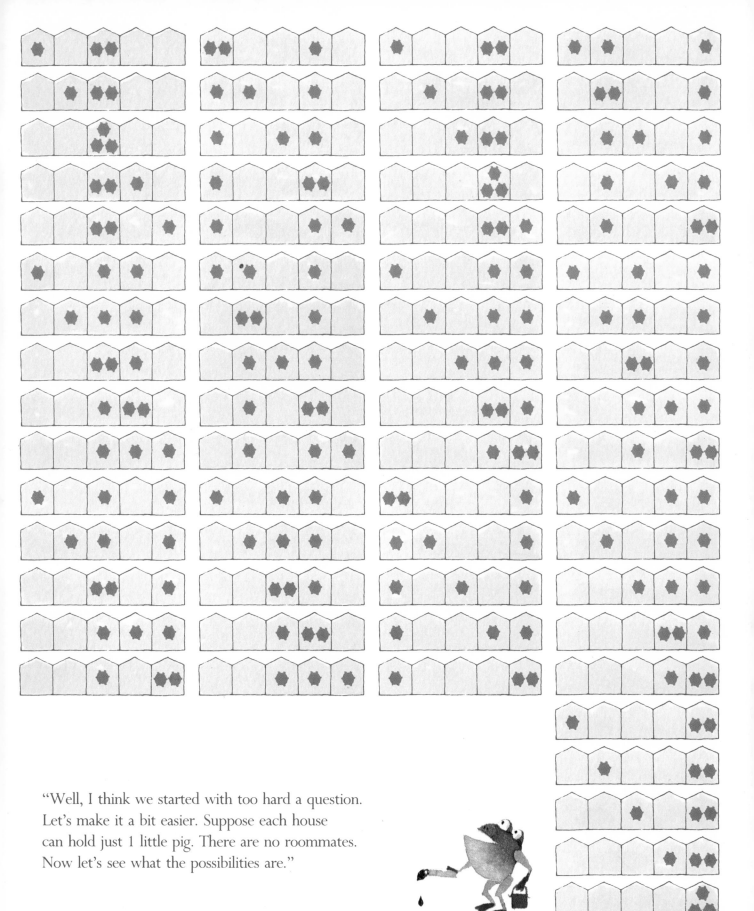

"Well, I think we started with too hard a question. Let's make it a bit easier. Suppose each house can hold just 1 little pig. There are no roommates. Now let's see what the possibilities are."

13

"All right. Here is the first little pig again. He has 5 choices,
just like before.

"He could be here

or here

or here

or here

or even here."

"Yes, but since there can be only 1 pig in each house, there are only 4 houses left for the second little pig to choose from.

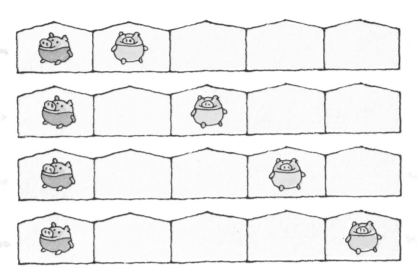

"It depends on where the first little pig is.

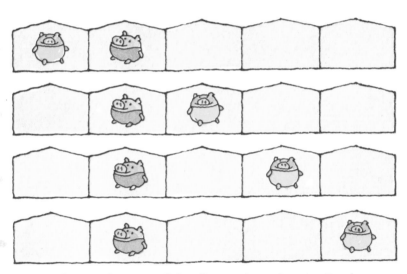

"Four choices for *each* of the first pig's 5 choices. So there are 4 times 5. That's 20 already!"

"Right, and the third little pig has just 3 choices, but remember, he also has 3 for each of the other arrangements, and there were 20 of those. It is still too hard for me, Pythagoras."

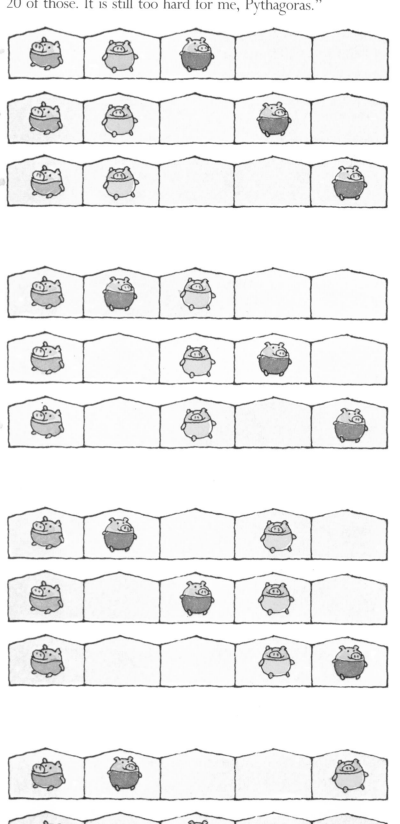

"Well, maybe it's easier to think of it as a tree again," said the frog.
"Each of the 5 big limbs is a house that the first pig could be in.
Then the 4 branches are the houses the second pig can choose from.
Then the 3 twigs are the possible choices of the third pig."

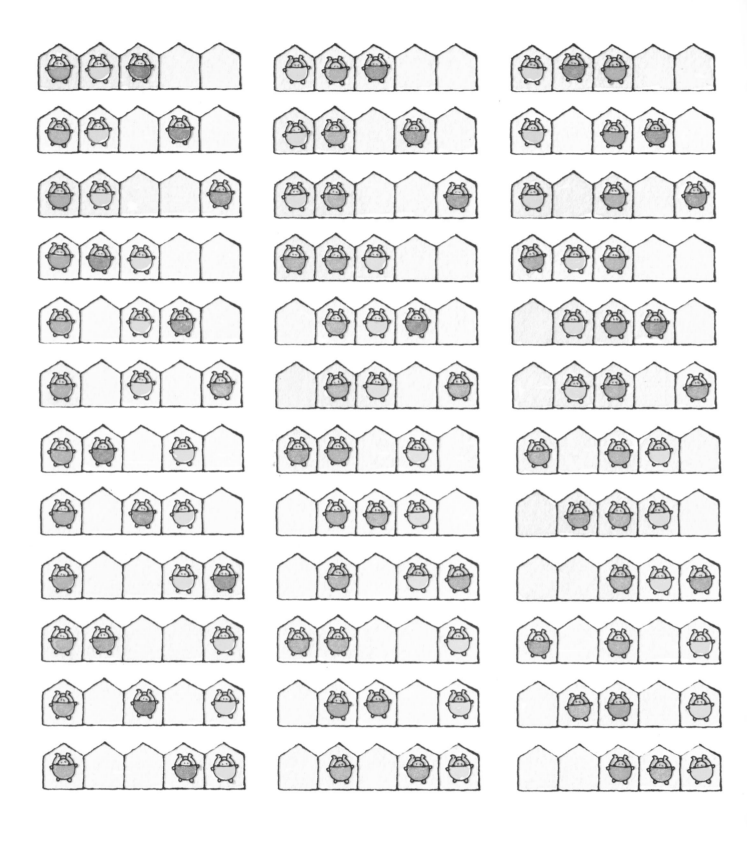

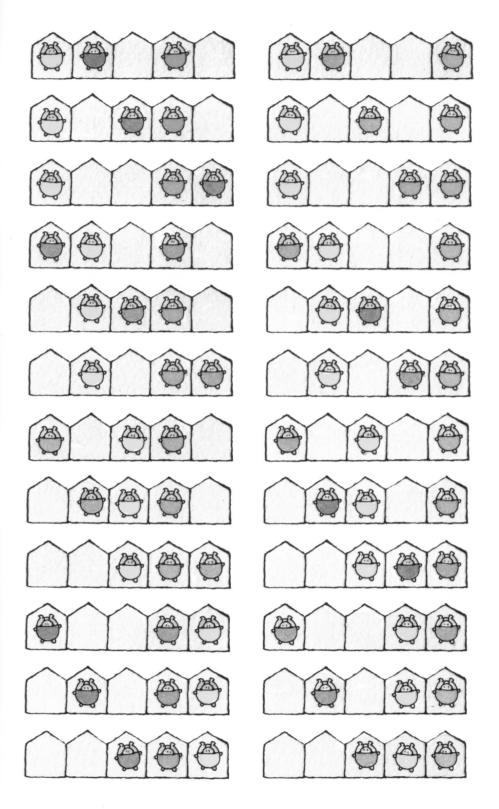

"So, 5 times 4 times 3—that's 60," said Socrates. "I'm going to draw them all out and look at them. It's better than 125, but it is still hard to know which pig is where. What do you think, Xanthippe, my dear?"

"I think you are wasting time," said Xanthippe crossly. "Who cares which pig you catch? They all taste alike in the dark, anyway."

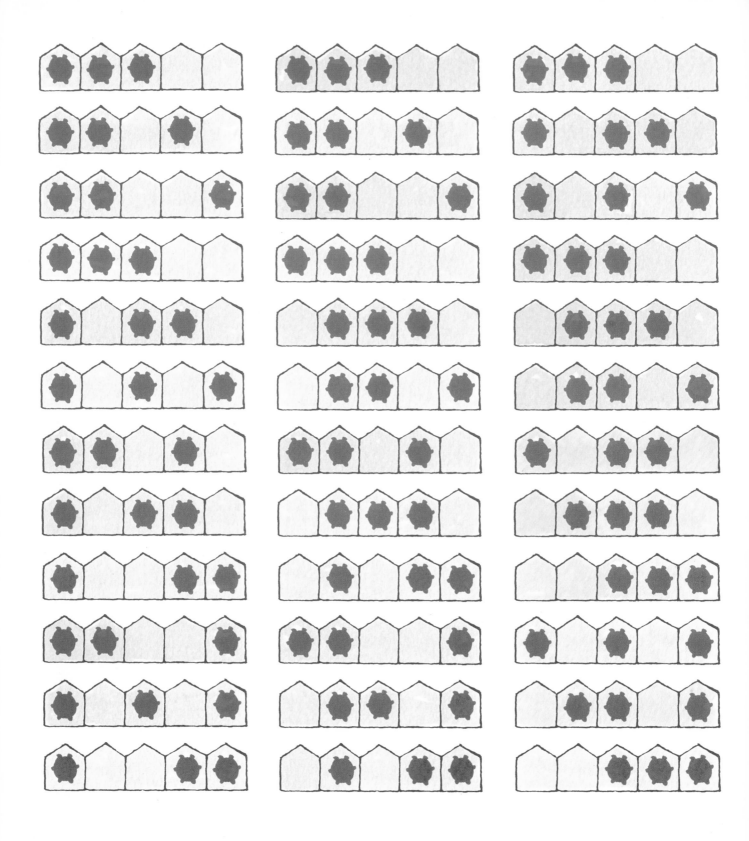

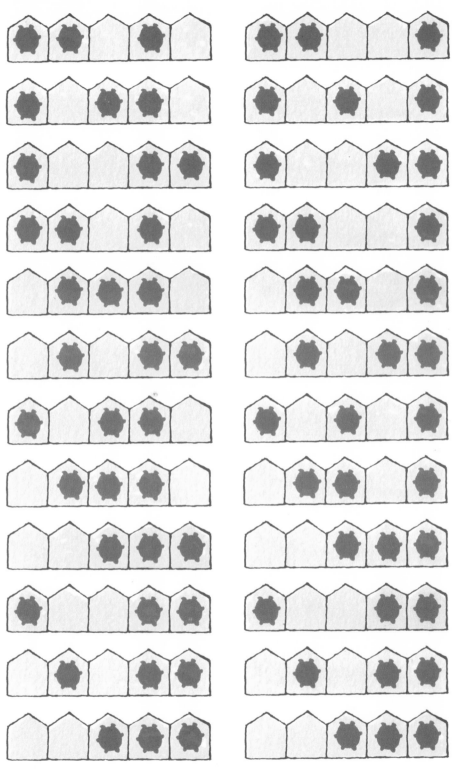

"Well, perhaps you are right. Let's make them all gray again and see if that makes it simpler. Look, now there are 6 each of 10 different arrangements. That does seem simpler. But why are they divided in sets of 6, Pythagoras?"

"Well, just think about it carefully. Suppose there are
3 chairs for our 3 little pigs."

"Chairs? But we were talking about houses, not chairs.
Oh, now I see. It doesn't really matter what we call it—
you just mean the place where the little pig *is.*
So now let's see where the first little pig can sit.

"He could sit here

or here

or here."

"Good. And now there are 2 choices for the second little pig.

There are still 6 different arrangements. But the third pig had only 1 possibility each time."

"And there are 2 choices here.

"And there are 2 choices here, too.

"Now the third little pig has only 1 possible chair to sit in, after the first two pigs have chosen theirs.

"So the total number of possible arrangements is 3 times 2 times 1, or 6."

"Correct! But do you really understand why? Let me show you
another tree, Socrates. Here are 3 limbs for the first pig's choices,
then 2 branches on each for the second pig's choices, and 1 leaf on
each branch for the third pig. You can count the leaves by ones,
and you'll get the same answer—6."

"Six possibilities!" shouted Xanthippe. "But if they're all colored gray, they all look alike!"

"That's right," said Pythagoras. "And that answers Socrates' question." (See page 21.)
"That's why each pattern was repeated 6 times. If they had 5 chairs to sit in, or 5 houses
to sleep in, they could arrange themselves in more different patterns, but each
pattern would still be repeated 6 times."

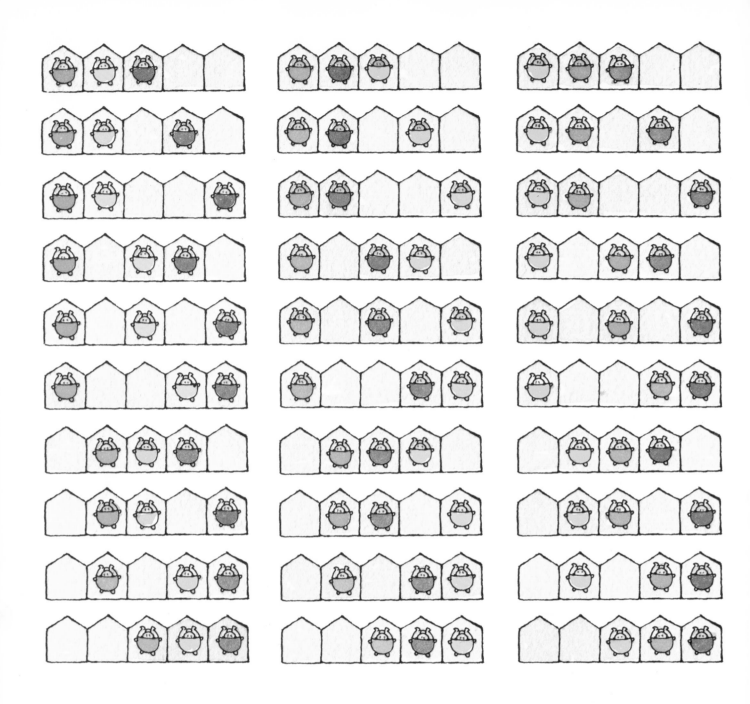

"Well," said Socrates, "I think I'd like to look at all *those* arrangements in an orderly way, too. That's how philosophers understand things. I've taken the 60 arrangements from pages 18 and 19 and put them into 6 columns.

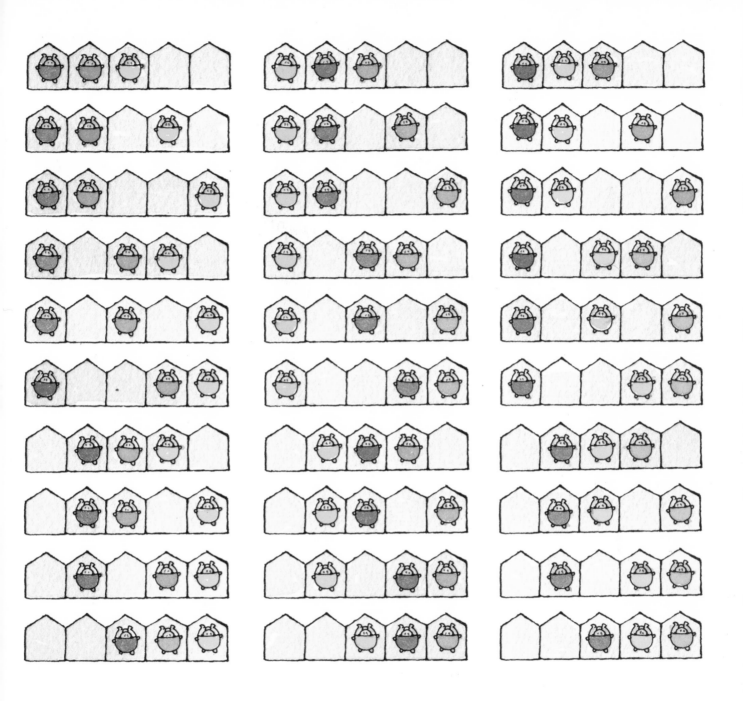

Reading *across* the page, you find the patterns are alike, if you don't bother about the colors. Reading *down* the columns, you can see 10 different patterns in each. So there are really only 60 divided by 6, or 10, different ways of combining the pigs in the houses! The problem is solved!"

"Very clever, Socrates! But you've only worked out the simple case where just one little pig is in a single house. What makes you imagine that they're not all living in *one* house?" Xanthippe rudely spat out a cherry pit as she spoke.

"To proceed from the simple to the complex is the goal of philosophy, my dear," replied Socrates. "So this time I will try to figure out all the possibilities. Let's see how the little pigs might be arranged inside the same house. What do you think of that, dear wifey?

"Here's the first little pig. This part is just as it was before.

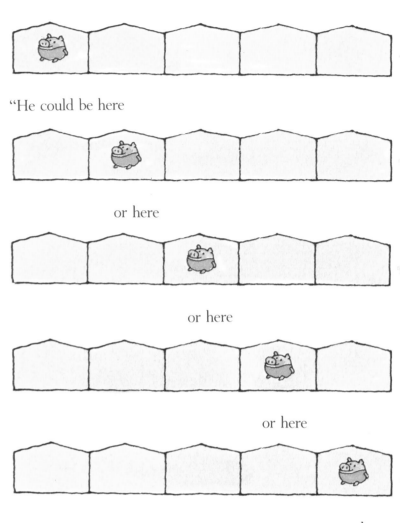

"He could be here

or here

or here

or here

or even here.

"This time the second little pig can go to the right or the left of the first little pig. So he has 1 more choice than before.

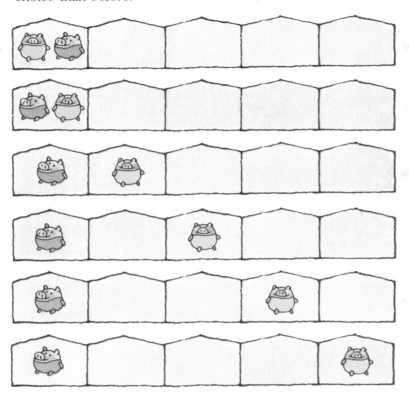

"For the second little pig there are 6 choices, one more than before.

"And for the third little pig there are 7 possible places, 2 more than before!"

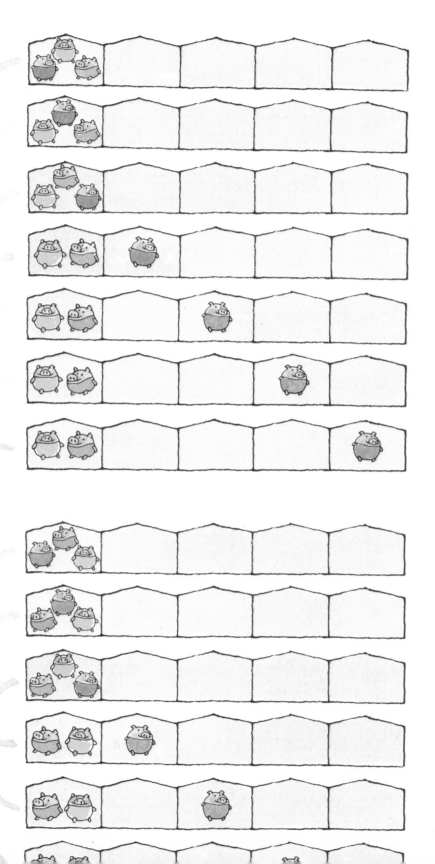

"Position matters in this example, as 1 pig might be closer to the door than the other. Then he would get caught first! For each choice by the first pig, the second pig has 6 possibilities, as the pictures show."

"I'll need to find a big, big tree to see how that looks," said Pythagoras.
"Each of the 5 big limbs has 6 branches and each branch has 7 twigs.
That's 5 times 6 times 7. How many is that in all, Socrates?"

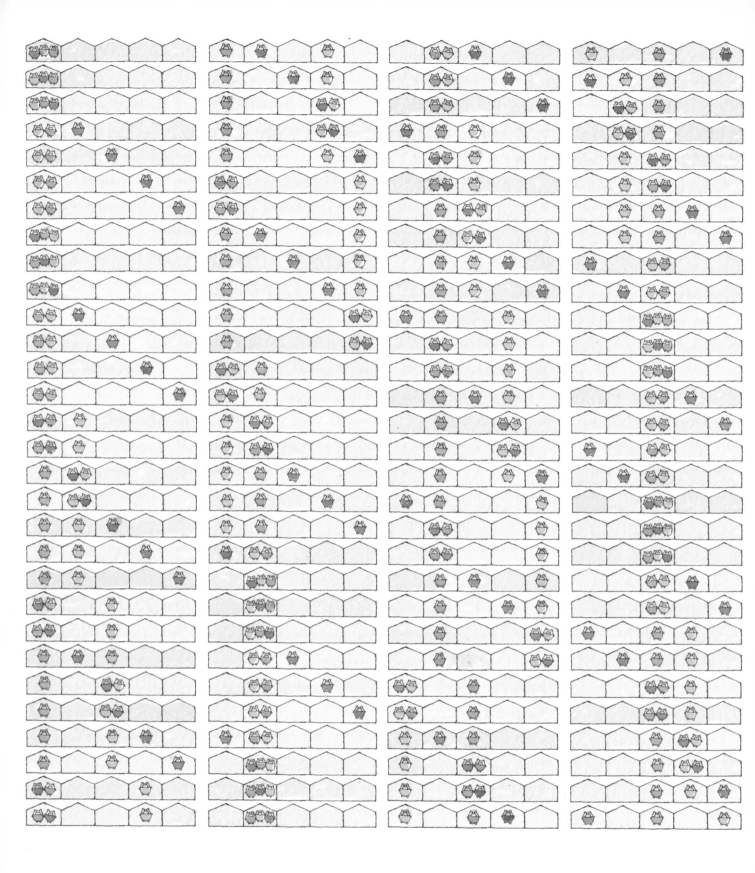

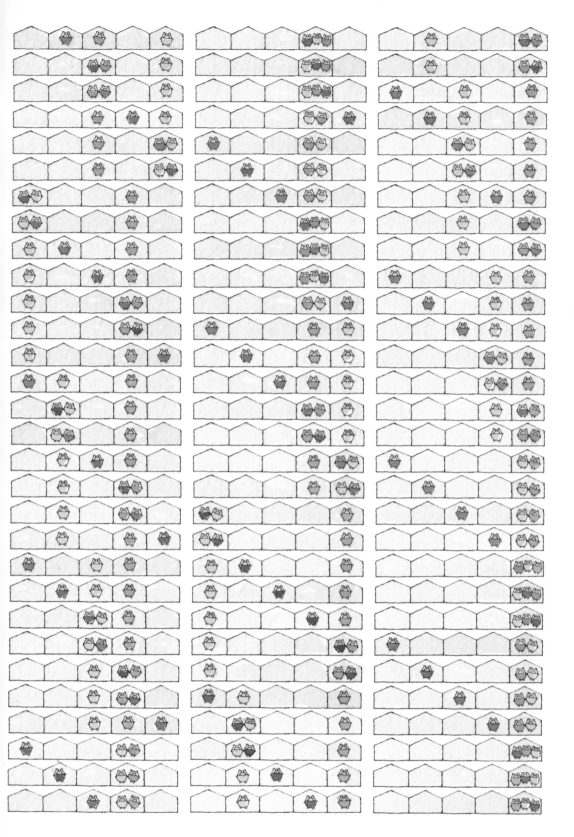

"Hm-m, 210. But you know I like to draw them all out and look at the piggies in their houses. Your trees are too plain for me. Just look how pretty my piggies are!"

"Pretty!" shouted Xanthippe. "Pretty *tasty,* too, I'll bet. Hurry up and color them all gray again, and let's see if that makes it easier to *catch* the pretty little things. I'm starving."

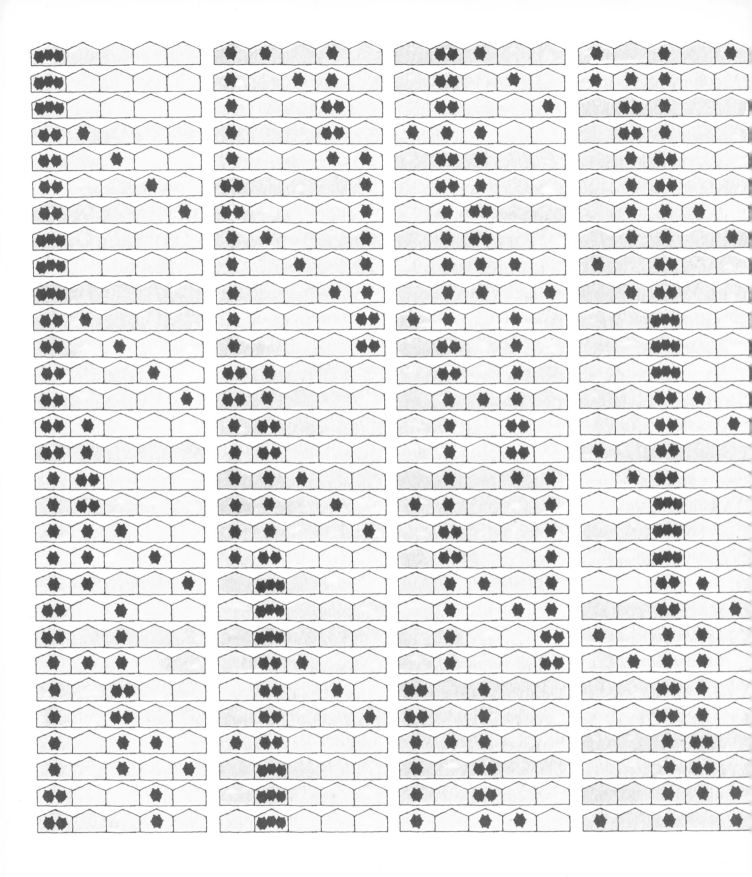

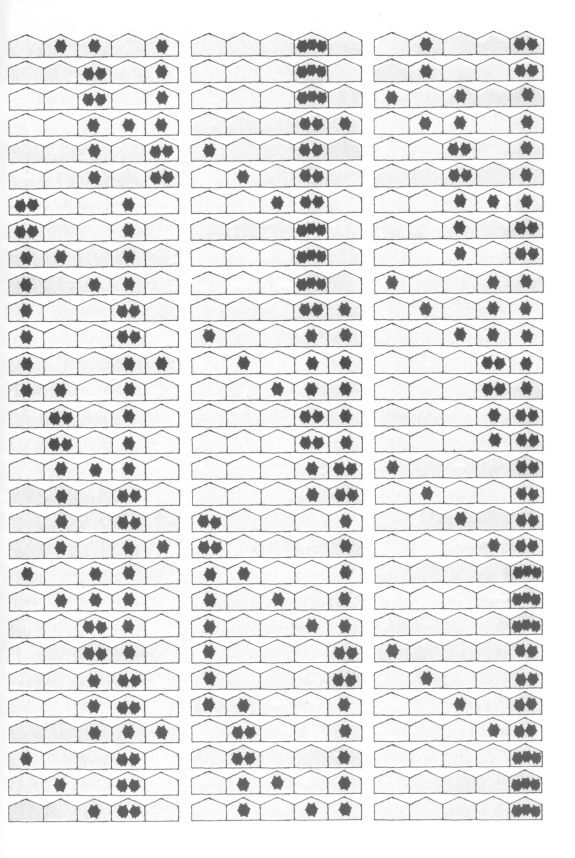

"Look, each pattern
is repeated 6 times,
just like before."

"Ah, you're just about
finished! Let's just pack
them in groups of 6
and eat them!"

37

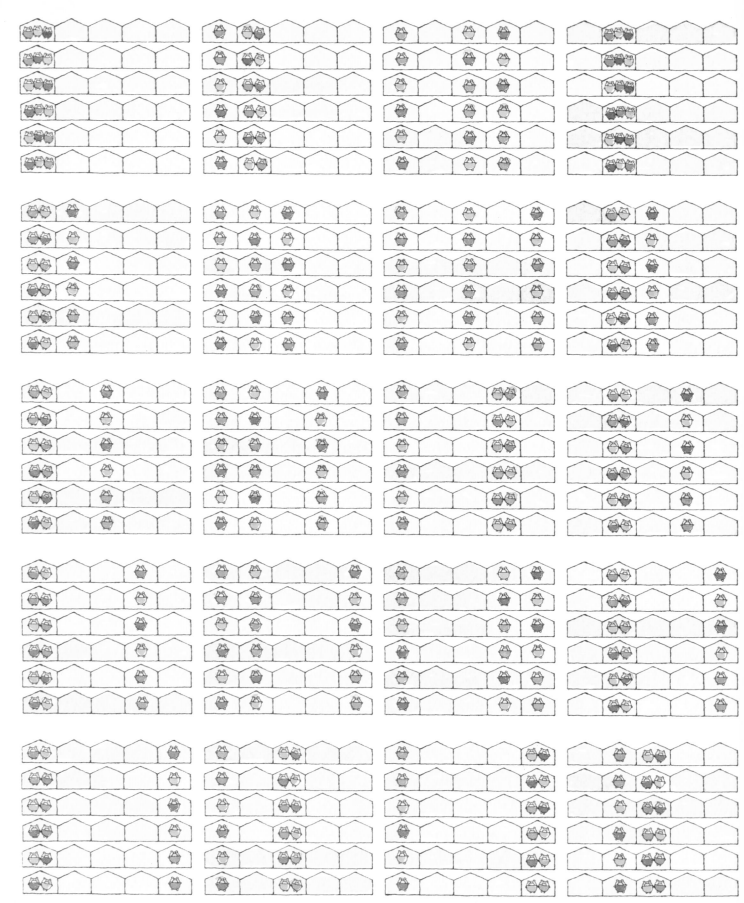

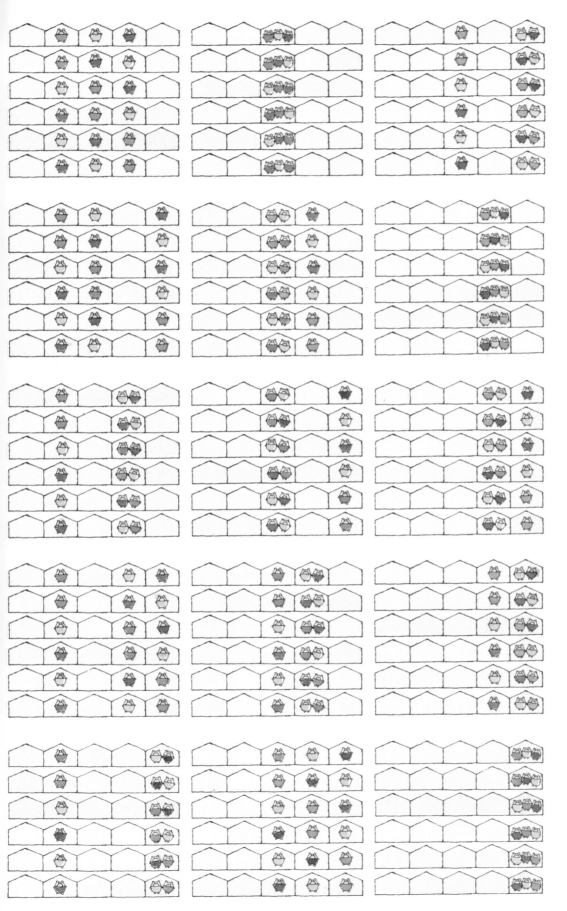

"Eureka! You've solved it, Xanthippe! 210 divided by 6 gives us 35 ways in which the 3 little pigs could be arranged in their 5 houses."

"Then let's go and catch them right away!" "Oh, no! It's too late! We've worked all night long, and it's daytime. The piggies are all out playing already."

39

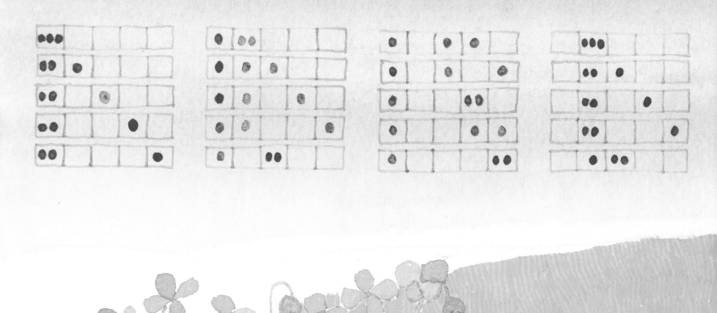

Socrates, Xanthippe, and Pythagoras looked out across the green
meadow. They saw the flowers aglow in the first rays of the morning
sun. They saw the 3 little pigs running and playing in the grass.
It was a peaceful scene. "How happy they look!" exclaimed Socrates.

"I don't think we should eat those nice little piggies, after all, do you?"
"Well, actually, I'm not hungry anymore," admitted Xanthippe.
"Then let's go play with them and be friends," said Socrates.
"Hurrah!" said Pythagoras. "That's the best solution of all!"

A Note to Parents and Other Older Readers

Although this book can be enjoyed just for the story and pictures, it has much more to offer than first meets the eye. For this is really an illustrated book about combinatorial analysis, mathematical permutations and combinations. However, the systematic and interrelated drawings and the thoughtful questions raised in the text allow even young children to explore the foundations of these advanced ideas.

Combinatorics, or combinatorial analysis, is one of the most useful concepts in modern mathematics—indeed, it might be said that the study of patterns and combinations *is* mathematics. Combinatorial analysis is a basis for computer programming, simplifying choices and showing not just *all* but also the *best* possibilities. It can be used in serious ways, such as in economic planning, or it can show you, for instance, the best routes to take when planning a holiday trip to multiple locations. It can tell you the probability that you will get a straight flush in your poker hand, or the chances that Socrates will find the piggie he wants in the first house he looks in. (Actually, in this book one cannot help suspecting that Socrates and Pythagoras may have used their lengthy exploration of the subject to *avoid* having to catch the charming little pigs for greedy Xanthippe to eat!)

At a higher level, mathematicians use convenient formulas for combinatorial analysis but often cannot explain their significance. In this book we have tried to make the underlying principles clear in pictures and words that can be understood by anyone who can count and do simple multiplication.

A permutation is any arrangement of the elements of a set *in a definite order*. For example,

suppose the three pigs decided to find all the ways that they could line up in groups of two. How many different arrangements could they form?

Designating the pigs as A, B, and C, we can form six groups of two:

AB, AC, BA, BC, CA, and CB

Notice that each arrangement can be paired with another that has the same elements: AB with BA, AC with CA, and BC with CB. But the members of each pair are *not* equivalent. For instance, the case of Pig A in front of Pig B is clearly not the same as that of Pig B in front of Pig A. The order does make a difference. Therefore we are dealing with permutations, and there are six.

In a combination, however, the order of the objects in an arrangement *does not matter*. For example, suppose the three pigs learn of Socrates' plot. Since they they are thinking animals just like the wolf, they decide to form a committee of two pigs (while one pig stands guard) to decide how to deal with the problem. How many different committees can they form?

In this problem, we are again forming arrangements of two elements from a set of three objects, so we can start by listing the same six permutations. But this time the pairs that have the same elements *are* equivalent. For instance, a committee of Pig A and Pig B is the same as a committee of Pig B and Pig A. So the six permutations are reduced to three identical pairs. The order in this sort of arrangement does not make a difference. Therefore we are dealing with combinations, and there are three.

This distinction between permutations and combinations is introduced throughout the text by Socrates' irritable wife Xanthippe, who points out that for her it does not matter which pig is chosen. Socrates, however, disagrees. He colors the pigs yellow, blue, and red to distinguish them. In effect he is looking for permutations. But when all the pigs are colored gray at his wife's request, he finds that many of the patterns are repeated. He is now looking at combinations, of which there are far fewer.

As parents and teachers discuss this book with children, they should encourage the youngsters to draw the various permutations for themselves. The task should be undertaken in a systematic fashion. If children lose track of the pattern, they can always refer to the pictures in the book to put them back on course. Children should also be encouraged to look for the multiple sets of each combination that appear on the pages where the pigs are darkened.

The story of Socrates and the three little pigs can be condensed into a simply stated question: In how many ways can 3 pigs be arranged among 5 houses? But Socrates is faced with many difficulties in determining the answer, because there is a great deal of important information that is not stated. Does it matter which pig is in a particular house or not (permutations or combinations)? Can more than 1 pig stay in a house? If more than 1 pig does stay in a house, does it matter how the pigs position themselves within the house?

At first Socrates explores the case in which more than 1 pig may enter a house, but without regard to the positioning of multiple pigs within a house. Socrates distinguishes the pigs by color. His pattern is started on pages 6 and 7 and developed in its entirety on pages 10 and 11. The first pig can go in any of the 5 houses. He has 5 choices. Each of those 5 choices also offers 5 options for the second pig (5 × 5, or 25, choices in all). Finally, each of those choices provides 5 options for the third pig. The tree diagram on page 9 visually demonstrates the mathematics: 5 sets of 5 sets of 5, or 5 × 5 × 5, or 125, permutations in all.

After children have had a chance to draw the permutations, parents may wish to give them the opportunity to study related cases. For example: How many permutations are there for 3 pigs among 4 houses? (4 × 4 × 4, or 64.) How many permutations are there for 2 pigs among 5 houses? (5 × 5, or 25.)

As the children study the combinations on pages 12 and 13, they should be encouraged to find multiple occurrences of particular patterns. There will be 6 pictures of each combination that contains 1 pig in a house, and 3 pictures of each combination that contains 2 pigs in a house. (There is only 1 picture, however, for each combination that contains 3 pigs in a house.)

Next, Socrates studies the case in which no more than 1 pig can stay in a house. Again, the first pig can go into any of the 5 houses; he has 5 choices. But this time each of those 5 choices offers only 4 options (5 × 4, or 20, choices in all) for the second pig, because he cannot go into a house that is already occupied. And from all of these arrangements, the third pig has just 3 choices, because 2 houses are already occupied. The tree diagram on page 17 depicts the mathematics: 5 sets of 4 sets of 3, or 5 × 4 × 3, or 60, permutations.

With the pigs darkened on pages 20 and 21, children will find that there are 6 occurrences of each combination. Anno shows why on pages 22 through 25: A combination of 3 pigs can be arranged in 6 ways.*

Now (page 29) Socrates charts himself a more complex situation. He decides to pay attention to how the pigs position themselves when 2 or more enter the same house. In drawing the possibilities, we find that the first pig again can choose any house and therefore has 5 choices. For the second pig things get a little more complicated. He can enter any of the 4 unoccupied cottages, or he can join the first pig; if he enters the occupied house he can go to either the left or the right of the other pig. Hence there are 2 options at the oc-

---

*On pages 12 and 13 not all the combinations can be arranged in 6 ways. This is because Socrates does not take into account the different positions that are possible when 2 or more pigs enter a house.